About the

J.E. Fahy is a 13-year-old author who wrote his first book at age 11. He lives in Galway, Ireland, with his parents, siblings and dog Luna. He enjoys writing stories, both long and short, and is constantly wondering what book to write next. He reads books for more writing styles and is constantly expanding on that subject. J.E. has many hobbies, which include reading, writing, soccer and brainstorming his million ideas.

J.E. Fahy

GLITCHED

AUSTIN MACAULEY PUBLISHERS™

LONDON · CAMBRIDGE · NEW YORK · SHARJAH

A CIP catalogue record for this title is available from the British Library.

ISBN 9781398441873 (Paperback)
ISBN 9781398441880 (ePub e-book)

www.austinmacauley.com

First Published 2022
Austin Macauley Publishers Ltd®
1 Canada Square
Canary Wharf
London
E14 5AA

Acknowledgements

My parents for always being there for me, encouraging me and always helping me.

My first teacher Ms Aisling for giving me encouragement.
My primary teacher Mùinteoir Grainne for saying my writing and ideas were always fabulous.
Kilbeacanty, Ballyturn and LKC, my schools and my parents, for teaching me to write.

Billì McFah is an Irish boy who grew up in Galway in a small, remote, tiny village. When he was nine, he and his family, Mamaì and Leasathair (mom and stepdad in Irish). His family only spoke Irish inside the house and outside it was English. And so, when An Era Nùa came, Billì knew exactly what it meant.

The New Era.

Chapter 1

Billì stood waiting in line. He brushed his dirty blonde hair out of his dark-brown eyes as he looked up at the door where kids went in but didn't come out. Two people left. One person left. Last person in, which meant…

'Billì McFah,' called the blonde lady at the door in a black tuxedo and tie.

Billì sighed. He hated needles.

'Coming,' he said and walked into the room.

The lady on the chair smiled at him. She had brown hair and grey eyes. A doctor motioned for Billì to lie on the bed in front of him.

'I'm Aoife Nodding, chair of An Era Nùa. Now, you're not going to remember this conversation and that's the only reason I'm telling you all this,' she said. 'Now, we're going to do an injection, which will make you feel like there is something under your skin. There will be nothing under it. There will, however, be a scab tomorrow morning. Do *not* pick at it, OK? Let it heal.'

Billì nodded. He was already told by other doctors and people like his parents not to pick at scabs, but the chair lady of The New Era? That was new!

Billì closed his eyes and let the doctor inject the thing that looked like a bead under his skin.

Wait! thought Billì. *Don't do—*

'It!' yelled Billì.

Mamaì stared at him with her blue eyes, her long black hair blowing in the wind that came from his bedroom window.

'You know you shouldn't yell random words at people,' she said in Irish. 'It makes no sense!'

'Sorry Mamaì,' Billì mumbled, also in Irish.

'I'm just so tired.'

'You must be,' Mamaì replied. 'The New Era brought you home on a stretcher.'

Billì sat up quickly. Quicker than usual, but Billì didn't think about that.

'The New Era?' he spluttered.

'Here?'

'Yes, now get changed before they come back and tie you to a tree,' she said, jokingly.

Billì slumped onto his bed.

Billì walked down the stairs, wide awake. Usually, Billì was always tired in the morning, but this morning he wasn't. Milly McFah stared at Billì with her piercing blue eyes, her black hair down to her waist and thought what to say.

Just then, Billì's head snapped upwards.

'Nanobot 127, Model 1.2.' Billì said in a robotic tone, 'All is in order. Minor glitch with camera and recording. Nothing to worry about. Soldier 127, out.'

Billì widened his eyes and stared back at Mamaì.

'I—I—I,' he stuttered. Mamaì didn't care he was speaking in English. Last time Billì had stuttered was when he was four and learning how to say the word Supercalifragilisticexpialidocious.

'What's wrong Billì?' asked Mamaì.

'I—I didn't want to say that,' he stuttered. 'I—I—I—I don't even know what I was talking about.'

'Maybe,' said Mamaì. 'We could go on holiday. Maybe go visit your dad's grave in Scotland, or your auntie in Wales, or even the London Bridge!'

'Can we do all of them?' asked Billì hopefully. Mamaì smiled, the subject successfully changed.

'Maybe.'

Chapter 2

And so Billì went to school the next day with a note to his teacher, Mrs Bellworth, about his trip to Britain and that he'd be going early at 12:00.

He left it on her desk and sat down.

Then, Aoife Nodding came into the room. Billì recognised her at once and nodded at her.

Aoife looked confused and stared at him.

The other kids, however, acted as if they never met her.

Then, Billì remembered what Aoife Nodding had said.

'I'm Aoife Nodding, chair of An Era Nùa. Now, you're not going to remember this conversation and that's the only reason I'm telling you all this.'

Billì wondered if she was behind all this. He decided not to take the chance and started whispering to everyone, asking if they knew her, looking puzzled.

Aoife… smiled.

She walked up to Mrs Bellworth's desk and turned to the class.

'Hello, everyone,' she said. 'Does anyone recognise me?' Billì was about to nod his head, then thought better of it and shook it.

Aoife pressed a button.

A voice in Billì's head suddenly turned on.

Stare right ahead, it said. *And only blink.*

Billì saw everyone else was doing it and did it.

Suddenly, he remembered something.

There had been a voice in his head that morning.

Say the following out loud. Nanobot 127, Model 1.2 it had said. *All is in order. Minor glitch with camera and recording. Nothing to worry about. Soldier 127, out.*

The voice had then stopped. Billì had had a dream the night before, in which a voice was ordering him to forget something about a needle and he was saying no and then some ones and zeros danced around and he woke up.

Aoife pulled out her phone.

'Attention all units, we have a glitch. One of the students nanobots are not responding and it seems that the student might not do what we say.'

Billì's mind raced. Nanobots? Glitch? Was she talking about him?

Then, she said something that answered his question. 'It's Nanobot 112 Model 1.1.'

Billì knew at once that Nanobot 112 wasn't him. He was Nanobot 127. Billì was about to sigh, then changed his mind; that would give him away.

He continued to stare ahead, as the voice was repeating that. It was getting annoying.

Stare ahead. Only blink. Stare ahead. Only blink.
Stare ahead. Only blink.
Stare ahead. Forget everything that was said and/or done while you were staring ahead.

'Why not? asked Billì dreamily.

Stare ahead. Forget everything that was said and/or done while you were staring ahead.

Why shouldn't I? Billì asked himself.

Stare ahead. Forget everything that was said and/or done while you were staring ahead.

Billì was about to allow himself to forget it, but stopped himself just in time.

Blink once.

Billì blinked once.

Go back to normal as if you woke up.

Billì did that, blinking, looking around, yawning.
'Well,' said Aoife. 'Now that we've had five minutes rest—'

'Five minutes?' whispered children everywhere. 'I don't remember anything.'

Then, a boy stood up. So did a girl.

Then, they ran through the window.

Without opening it.

Chapter 3

12:00.

Billì put up his hand.

'Umm… Eva?' he asked.

Aoife looked at him.

'Eva… Stocking?' he asked. Children around him laughed.

'I'm Aoife Nodding… Bill,' she said.

'Sorry,' said Billì. 'I forgot.' Aoife smiled.

'Of course, you did,' she said.

Aoife turned to the door as two men walked through it. They had tuxedos and silver briefcases. They walked over to the window and started dusting the window.

Ignore them.

Billì stared at them.

Ignore them.

'Billì?' asked a voice distantly.

Billi continued staring.

'Attention all units. We have a glitch.'

'Billì!'

Billì sat up. He was in a car.

His heart started beating hard. How did he get in there? Why was he in the car? Who was driving—

'You awake sweetie?' asked Mamaì.

Billì nodded. 'Yeah. What happened?'

'I came at 12 and saw you asleep on your desk. Some men were checking your pulse and I pulled you up and brought you into the car.

'I explained all that to Aoife, that nice woman who was subbing, that we were just going home to unpack. If you're sick at school, then—'

'Mamaì!' said Billì. 'I thought we were going on a trip!'

'We are.' Mamaì winked. Billì smiled. Mamaì had outsmarted an evil woman without thinking.

Billì heard a voice in his head; *Tracking mode enabled.*

Billì started, then had an idea.

If he could ignore the voice, could he disable the tracking mode? Billì decided to give it a try. Something was fishy, and it wasn't Mamaì`s car.

Disable tracking mode.

Billì smile widened. Maybe there was a control room.

Activate spy through camera mode.

Billì thought for a second. Control room camera? Nah.
There's a load of those. AEN cameras? Maybe…

AEN control room camera.

State password.

Billì tensed.

12326?

Silence.

Then…

Lockdown mode initiated. Strength, Speed and Stamina down. SCM firewall activated. AEN intruder alarm—

Disabled! Billì ordered quickly, sweaty.

AEN intruder alarm disabled. Doors unlocked. Windows open. Computers on.

Lockdown lasted: 1.0009 seconds. Strength Speed and Stamina back up.

Billì waited. And waited.

But SCM (Spy-Camera Mode) firewall never came down.

Chapter 4

As Billì was resting after putting all his bags in the car, a boy ran up to him, put a note and a notepad in his hand and ran off.

Billì stared after him. All he could see was brown hair. He put the notebook in his pocket and read the note.

He put the note in his pocket. A man in a tuxedo walked up to him too.

Answer him truthfully.

'Did a boy walk past?' the man asked.
Billì nodded.
'Did he give you anything?' Billì nodded.
'Can I have it please?'

Give it to him. Give it to him. Give it to him.

Billì gave the crumpled-up piece of paper to the man.
The man nodded, smiled and brought it away.
Billì shook his head as if he was coming out of a trance and walked into the car.
Billì sat on his seat B1 and he took out the note.

He read it, but everything on it was lines.

He took out the notepad and saw it explained all the lines on the note and other words, like a dictionary.

He imagined Aoife's expression when she saw that the paper was just a shopping list.

Billì chuckled and nearly didn't notice the voice in his head.

Of course, if you ever had a voice in your head, you'll know it's hard to ignore it.

SCM firewall disabled.

Billì listened, then had an idea.

State password and suspected hacker.

Grand, a Runner with Gretel Billìon, who are thought to be in England.

Billì smiled and threw his head back. It was handy being able to know all the enemies' passwords.

Activate SCM. Password: 123P325R. England cameras.

Flick one by one. Linger on each one for three seconds. Scan faces for Gretel Billìon and Bran Grand.

London Bridge had nothing. Big Ben, nothing. Nothing. Nothing. Nothing. Gretel.

Stop!

Go back to camera C1 23.

Camera C1 23.

Billì stared through it and saw Gretel, a girl with blonde hair and green eyes, putting food in her backpack and, after pulling at Bran, the boy with brown eyes and brown hair that had given Billì the note and notepad, go into a house.

Billì nodded. An abandoned house.

State address of that house.
No address known.
All is known is that it is 125 metres from London Bridge.

Deactivate SCM.

Deactivating SCM.
Uploading orders and camera footage to AEN main computer.
Cancel upload!

Upload cancelled.

Billì started to sweat. Did all the proof that his nanobot wasn't working uploaded?

Was he going to be the person getting Gretel and Bran found? Was he going to be a—

'What would you like?' asked the person pushing the food trolley.

'Crisps. Salt and Vinegar. Please. Thanks. Here's €2. Keep the change,' he said.

The woman pushing the trolley went to the next person.

After eating all his crisps and drinking some water, Billì knew he wasn't going to enjoy the trip if he kept on worrying about Bran and Gretel.

So, he closed his eyes and relaxed.

Chapter 5

Billì sighed happily. He had visited Big Ben and the Parliament Building so far and today was the day for London Bridge. He had walked down and was walking back up when he remembered that 125 metres from where he was were Bran and Gretel.

'Mamaì?' asked Billì. 'Can we go to get an ice cream? It's hot.'

It was hot, but not so hot for ice cream, but luckily Mamaì agreed. Billì said he would wait for her at the bridge.

Mamaì agreed again and went to look for an ice cream shop. Billì knew Mamaì would never give up on something she had her mind set on and that there wasn't an ice cream shop anywhere near the bridge.

So off he went.

Billì counted the 125 metres and ended up in front of a dark alleyway.

He looked around and what he saw made him jump.

Men in tuxedos with the AEN symbol on it running towards him.

Billì ran down the bridge away from the men. He looked over his shoulder and saw them smiling, their golden AEN badges glinting in the sun.

Before he could be confused, he ran right into another man, grinning and flashing his AEN badge.

As he looked around looking for an escape route he felt a hand on his arm, pulling him into a bin.

He saw a boy pressing a button and then the boy was gone, running through a dark tunnel.

Billì ran after him.

As Billì ran and ran, he realised he had been saved by Bran Grand, the bin was a secret passage and that he was going to meet Gretel Billìon.

'Who are you?' asked Bran as they fell.

'Billì,' said Billì. 'How's life Bran?'

Bran grinned. 'Am I famous?'

'To An Era Nùa, definitely,' said Billì.

'You on the run? asked Bran.

'Sort of,' said Billì.

'Runner, Forgotten or Glitched? asked Bran.

'Umm…'

'Oh, right, you don't know what those things are!' exclaimed Bran. 'Well, a Runner is someone who never got a nano bot and is on the run. A Forgotten is someone who never got an appointment, meaning that they were forgotten, hence the name. And a Glitched is someone whose nanobot isn't working. They're able to ignore it and control it and they have the strength, speed and stamina that the nanobot gives you.'

'The nanobot gives you all that?' asked Billì.

'Yup,' said Bran.

Billì stared at his arm. He looked at Bran and lifted him up with his pinkie.

'I think I'm a Glitched,' Billì said casually.

'Me too,' said Bran.

Billi put him back on the ground, they looked at each other and burst out laughing.

Gretel walked out and looked at Billi.

She smiled. 'I'm gonna like this one.'

Billì stood up and shook Gretel's hand.

'I'm Billì,' he said. 'Nice to meet you, Gretel.'

Gretel giggled.

Then another Gretel came out through the door.

'Ah,' said Gretel. 'Bran, explain to him.'

'Yes Gretel,' Bran said. 'Gretel and Hansel are twins. That's Hansel, the younger one that's always laughing and that's Gretel, the older one that is and always will be boss of SOW.'

'SOW?' asked Billì.

'Save Our World,' explained Bran. 'We're always on the move, getting Runners, Forgottens and Glitches.

When we're on the brink of being found—'

'Cancel camera request. Cancel recording request,' interrupted Hansel.

'—which is when that happens, we move. We're going to Scotland next,' continued Bran as if nothing happened.

Billì nodded. 'Sooooo what are you guys?'

'Glitched,' said Hansel.

'Runner,' said Bran.

'Forgotten,' said Gretel.

'I'm a Glitched too!' said Billì.

'Forgotten,' said a voice.

Instinctively, Billì ducked, kicked behind him and held someone to the ground.

'Urgh,' said the person.

24

Billì stood up, dusted himself and caught a punch coming from the person.

He had black hair and yellow eyes.

Billì looked at the fist.

'Oh, great,' he muttered.

'Aoife went to secondary schools too?'

'Who?' everyone asked.

'I know!' Billì said. 'I'll ask for a file of her!'

File for Aoife Nodding. Say it out loud.

'Aoife Nodding,' said Billì.

'Chair of An Era Nùa, orphan, 21 years old, blue eyes, blonde hair, founder of NNB, New Nano Bots.'

Billì stopped himself. Her file went on for a while.

'That's her,' he said.

Gretel and Bran said, 'I remember her!' The unnamed boy still didn't know her but recognised her from the school and Hansel didn't.

Hansel just cried.

Billì looked at her with a confused look and Bran saw it.

'She has Gretel's nanobot,' Bran said. 'So, she has double the power, but it's harder to resist it and she doesn't remember anything about the week before she got the nanobot. We thought it wouldn't be permanent, but...'

'Maybe she just needs a bigger memory sparker to get her memory back,' suggested Billì. Hansel smiled at that.

Billì knew he had to go.

'I have to go, my mom will be looking for me,' said Billì.

Hansel and Bran nodded, the still unnamed boy shrugged, but Gretel shook her head.

'That's the first place they'll think you are, you know that,' she said.

'Which is exactly why they'll check there last,' replied Billì as he ran through the secret passage.

Gretel smiled. That boy wasn't as bad as the other two.

Then, she walked back to the house to plan their route out of England.

Chapter 6

To anyone watching, they saw a teenage woman sneeze into her tissue, put it in her hand and walk around, looking for a bin.

To anyone who was looking for anything suspicious might notice she was only a few feet away from a bin.

To an advanced person looking for anything suspicious, might notice that a bin was five feet away from her and that the tissue got a tiny bit bigger than any other tissue would. To an even more advanced than advanced person, such as one of The Triplette B, would notice all that and that she was wearing very tall high heels, high heels that only people wanting to look taller would wear. And that she was walking suspiciously wobbly, as if it was her first time in high heels.

So, The Triplett B followed her.

As you may have guessed, that woman wasn't a woman. It was Billì.

Billì had taken out a rock and a sharp piece of metal. He had scratched a note in the code the SOW used, saying:

Grounded cannot meet, go to Scotland you're being watched.

He had donned his disguise, walked up to London Bridge and acted like a regular tourist. Which was pretty good for a 12-year-old.

But not good enough to fool the Triplette B.

The Triplette B were Italian triplets, all of them had a name beginning with B. The triplets were trained assassins, trackers and secret billionaires.

Take any famous rich person, look up how much money they have and double it. Then double it again. That was how much the Triplett Bs had.

They had the best guns, daggers, gear, and they were expensive.

Add all those together and you have a successful silent black-market business of assassinations and making you very, very rich.

Billì looked in his make-up mirror and saw them behind him. He gulped.

Scan and identify.

Bayne Barden. Bill Barden. Boru Barden. The Triplette B. The Silent Suiciders. The Angry Assassins. The Demons of Hell. The Di—

Stop! Give me ID's.

Bayne Barden. Strength is his main strength, but he is good with a pistol. Bill Barden.

Speed and pinpoint accuracy are his main strength, but with his shoe only he could have you on the floor, dead.

Boru Barden. The brains of the whole operation. Never laugh at his name, he could convince you to commit suicide with just his eyes.

Billì gulped. He saw the bin and smiled. He turned on his voice changer.

'Finally, a bin!' he exclaimed, sounding exactly as a teenage girl would.

Billì saw Bayne and Bill look at Boru, who didn't keep his eyes off Billy's head.

All of them had black hair and grey eyes and pale skin, like a vampire.

Billì shuddered.

Billì threw the paper in the bin.

'And she scores!' he said, pretending to be a commentator. 'And the crowd goes - whoa!'

Billì stared at them and instantly wished he hadn't bought the necklace and went with the eye colour changing contacts.

'Who are you guys?' he purred.

'Lady why are you wearing a wig?' asked Boru.

Billì hung his head.

'I guess I've been caught. You can arrest me now.'

Boru looked at her in confusion and edged out his tranquiliser gun.

'I…' Billì sighed. 'I'm bald.' Boru blinked, then burst out laughing.

'I thought you were that Bill-e guy we're looking for.' Boru grinned. Behind him Bayne and Bill grinned too.

'Who?' asked Billì, pretending to be puzzled.

'Oh, Bill-e McFa. He's a criminal. Ran from school and took a plane all the way to England. His mother's worried sick.'

'Oh, McFah!' Billi laughed.

'Silly me. I saw Mrs McFah in the restaurant yesterday with her son, a boy called Billy.

Nice chap. Are Billy and Bill-e twins?'

Boru nodded. 'Got it in one.' He lied, obviously. Billì walked past Boru and Bill and said, 'I'll tell Mrs McFah that her son is being found by you nice men now.'

Bayne walked in front of Billì. Boru shook his head.

'I'm afraid we can't have that, Billì.' Boru chuckled. 'Almost got me, until I saw your hair behind that wig. Curly hair is really hard to hide under a wig, you know.'

Billì whipped off the wig, slid under Bayne's legs and ran off. He kicked off the high heels, took aim and hit Bayne and Bill in the face. Boru nodded.

'Impressive,' he said as he took out a sniper rifle. 'Now, I usually let Bill do the shooting, but he's out, so—'

Boru was now on the ground, unconscious, a tranquiliser dart in his arm.

Billì smiled. Boru had taken his eyes off one of the fastest and strongest kids in the world, with excellent stamina. He hadn't stood a chance. Billì turned on his heel and ran home.

Chapter 7

'Billì!' yelled Leasathair. 'Billì!' Billì walked into the sitting room of the apartment they were renting.

Where else would they be staying in England?

'Yes Jack?' mumbled Billì. He glanced at the clock. It was five o'clock in the morning.

'It's five o'clock in the bloody morning!' yelled Leasathair.

His red hair was sticking everywhere and his green eyes were full of rage.

'I can see that,' mumbled Billì.

'And YOU woke me up!' he continued.

Billì rolled his eyes. Classic Leasathair, trying to get him into trouble.

'I believe you woke *me* up,' he said. 'You were the one who yelled at me to come downstairs.'

Leasathair stared at Billì.

'Listen, young man,' growled Leasathair. 'I am your stepdad—'

'I know,' said Billì.

Leasathair had closed his eyes.

'Your father is dead, your mother asleep, you have no friends and no siblings here and you are being sarcastic to me?' roared Leasathair.

Then…

He opened his eyes. Billì put up his hand, caught Leasathair's fist, twisted it, let go, jumped in the air, spinning, came down and kicked Leasathair in the face.

Then he flipped backwards, landed on his feet and dusted his hands.

Billì realised something.

I can sense things. Leasathair glared and ran towards Billì again.

Cool!

Billì slid under Leasathair's legs and turned around. He smiled at Leasathair.

'I could do this with my eyes closed,' he said.

Leasathair grinned. 'Do it then,' he growled.

And Billì closed his eyes.

He caught and blocked kicks and punches, hit his target with his own and took down Leasathair again. And again.

And again.

When Leasathair started to pant, Billì opened his eyes. All around him, knives and forks were stuck to the wall, looking like they were aimed at him.

Billì gulped but turned to Leasathair with a friendly smile.

'You do know you can just ask me to leave,' joked Billì. 'And also, I think that killing your stepson is illegal.'

Leasathair looked up, confused.

'But your—' Leasathair straightened himself up and shook his head. 'It doesn't matter. It seems you are sick.

Crazy. You attacked your stepfather. I'm afraid I may have to ask AEN to… look after you. Don't you agree, Milly?'

Billì looked at Mamaì. She was white with shock and fear.

But, slowly, she nodded her head.

She turned to Billì.

'It's for the best,' she whispered.

Chapter 8

And Billì was now on the run from the police, his family and more importantly, AEN.

He had just deleted Tracking Mode in his nano-bot and was just finishing packing when Mamaì came into the room.

Mamaì looked at him in horror.

'Billì!' she said. 'You can't run away!'

'An Era Nùa will do bad things to me Mamaì,' he replied, as he shoved some socks into his bag.

'Not to help me, but to control me.'

Billì stood up.

'N—no,' Mamaì said and she stood in the doorway. 'You're not walking through this here door. Not now, not ever.'

Billì shook his head.

'Wasn't planning to,' he said. Then, he turned to the window and, without opening it, jumped out. And fell 15 floors.

'Impressive,' said Bran.

The group were watching the replay of Billì jumping out of his window 15 floors high on their old black and white TV they had found in a skip.

Gretel sighed. 'Just to get away from AEN,' she said.

'His body wasn't found, though,' said Bran. 'Maybe he survived.'

It was a week since Billì had jumped out the window and Bran, Gretel, Hansel and the other boy were packing. They were leaving for Scotland.

'Bran,' said Gretel, putting a hand on his shoulder. 'No one could have survived that.'

'Survived what?' asked a voice.

The group jumped and turned to see a figure walking towards them.

'Well,' said Gretel, bringing her fists up. 'I'm not going down without a fight.'

She let out a yell and ran at the figure.

The figure stopped walking, grabbed Gretel's fist and looked at it.

'You're getting better Gretel,' the figure said. 'A bit more to the left, though and maybe use your leg too and if I was an AEN, I'd be on the floor.' Gretel blinked, then laughed.

'Merry, stop fooling around!' She grinned.

The figure walked into the room and pulled off her disguise.

She had blonde hair and yellow eyes and freckles.

'I thought it was pretty good,' said the boy-who-we-still-don't-know-what-his-name-is.

'Thanks, Sam,' said Merry, smiling at the boy (Finally, we know what his name is

Sam smiled back.

'So,' Merry said. 'Bob has contacts at Blackpool. They'll get you to Lanark right away. Where are you going in Lanark exactly?'

'Yeah,' said a voice in the secret passage. 'Where exactly?'

Merry looked over her shoulder, then back to Gretel.

'No one else was with me when I came,' she whispered.

'I double checked before I went into the passage.'

'Well, it's really easy to get into a passage that you know about,' said Billì, stepping into the room.

Merry dropped her walkie talkie in shock of seeing a boy who jumped 15 floors walking and talking in front of her.

Chapter 9

Terry took out her walkie talkie. She had blonde hair and red-orange eyes.

'Harry, Barry,' she whispered into it. 'Merry went into the entrance and then a boy followed her. She's not answering her walkie talkie.'

'Take out your grenades,' said a voice through the walkie talkie. 'I'm sending Barry right now.'

Terry smiled.

'Thanks,' she said and ran into the bin, taking out her grenades as she went.

Bran stared at Billì.

Merry nodded.

'You're strong,' said Gretel. Billì rolled his eyes.

'Finally, after I take down the Triplette B, lift Bran in the air, jump 15 floors and survive it. You think I might be a little strong?' said Billì sarcastically.

'Well, not really strong anyway,' said Bran.

Everyone laughed, apart from Merry, who had frozen in shock.

Billì looked at her.

'What's wrong?' he asked. Merry turned to him.

'W—what do you mean, the Triplette B?' she asked.

'Bill, Bayne and Boru,' Billì said. 'Why?'

'S—s—so Boru was there? And his brothers?' she asked.

'Which other Triplette B is there?' Billì asked.

'Merry,' Bran said. 'What's wrong?'

'We have to get the hell out of here!' she said. 'Now!' Someone started clapping.

Slowly.

Then, Terry was thrown into the room, with a big man on top of her. The man had brown hair and black eyes.

Merry ran over to the two people.

'Terry? Barry?' she whispered. The man (Barry) leaped up, his black eyes full of rage, as the still clapping man came into the room. Boru.

Chapter 10

Bill and Bayne walked in and cuffed the group together in a circle.

'Well done,' Boru said. 'For staying under the radar for sooooo long. But the truth always gets out in the end. STW, SOW, AEN, DAB, we all know what they stand for—'

'Daniel And Brothers?' Terry said suddenly. 'What do they have to do with this?'

Boru rolled his eyes and, for a while, looked like he was thinking, but eventually he shrugged.

'Sponsors AEN,' he said with a dismissive wave of his hand.

'Now, let's have you all scheduled because you are all sick.' He glared at all of them.

'All of you.'

Bill and Bayne looked at each other.

'I don't feel sick,' they said at the same time.

Boru turned to them.

Big mistake.

'No, not you, them!' Boru said, turning around and pointing at the handcuffed group.

Bayne and Bill nodded. Bayne pointed to the boy beside Boru.

'Even him?' he asked.

Boru looked at where Bayne was pointing and Sam punched him in the face, knocking him unconscious.

Bill and Bayne groaned.

They looked at Boru, who glared at them.

'What's wrong Boru?' asked Bayne.

Bill looked at their wrists.

'I think we are handcuffed,' he said.

'WE ARE!' yelled Boru. 'THE CHILDREN AND THE TWO ADULTS GOT AWAY!!!'

Bill and Bayne covered their ears.

'You're loud Boru,' said Bill.

'OF COURSE, I AM!!! YOU FAILED!!!' yelled Boru.

Terry and Merry picked some disguises for the members of SOW to wear as the SOW and Barry walked around the brick factory (aka the STW base).

'Sooooo we're going to an abandoned house?' Billì asked, rolling his eyes. 'Is it your thing, abandoned places?'

'No,' said Gretel. 'Then we'd be going somewhere else.' Billì nodded. 'Good point.'

Merry and Terry came into the room.

'The rest of us will be at Lanark,' Merry said.

'Come on, hurry up, AEN are around the corner,' said Terry.

'What?' asked Merry.

'I saw their van,' Terry explained. 'Let's go!'

And with that, SOW and the three members of STW went into the private jet on the driveway.

Chapter 11

A few minutes later, the SOW and STW arrived in Lanark.

Billì sat down in the pillow factory where Harry, a man with black hair and brown eyes, was waiting for them.

Harry sat in the driver seat of his red Ford Fiesta and drove off with the SOW while Merry and Terry continued to fly in the jet.

'To make them think you're still on the jet,' explained Harry.

'They'll put it to auto-pilot soon and jump out into a taxi driven by Bob and he'll drop them off with Steve.' Harry winked. 'Or that's what AEN will see. It's actually some actors that are told this is all some part of a movie and they will be the people jumping out.'

Billì nodded, then smiled.

'Smart,' he said. 'And kinda confusing.'

'Thanks,' said Harry. 'Came up with the plan myself.'

Billì nodded. He was beginning to see the people of STW's roles…

Bob – contacts (as in people, not the bits of plastic you put in your eyes to see better).

Merry – disguises.

Terry – explosives.

Barry – fights.

Harry – plans.

'What will Mairì be doing?' Asked Sam.

'Mairì?' Billì asked. 'Who's Mairì?'

'Mairì made the bin secret entrance,' said Bran.

Billì put Mairì on the list.

Mairì – inventions.

'We're here,' said Harry.

Very quickly, the SOW double-checked their disguises, opened the car door and walked outside, towards the abandoned house that would be their base.

When Billì opened the door, a wind came from inside, blowing off their disguises.

Hands pulled them inside. When Billì looked up, he saw, over him, was an unmistakable face.

'Hello, Billì,' said Aoife Nodding. 'You have an overdue appointment.'

Billì suddenly felt an urge to punch her, but a voice told him not to and to his horror, he did something he believed he would never do.

Don't hit her Billì.

Why would I?

Billì was listening to his nano-bot.

Book Two of the Amazing Series!

Unknown

Join Billi and SOW as they travel through Scotland, on the run from the evil AEN. Will they survive? Only one way to find out…